Fly Away Home

'You'll be OK now,' I said to the eggs. 'I promise. Your mum's not here but you're going to be OK . . .'

Amy Alden finds a nest of goose's eggs and brings them home. The baby geese follow her all the time – they think she is their mother. Now the geese must fly south for the winter. Amy and her dad must help them fly away home . . .

Many people saw the film *Fly Away Home* with Anna Paquin as Amy Alden and Jeff Daniels as her father. The story is about the work of a Canadian, Bill Lishman. With a small aeroplane, he helped his geese fly from Canada to the USA.

Patricia Hermes writes books for children and young people. She wrote *Mama Let's Dance*, *On Winter's Wind* and *The Cousins Club*. She also wrote books about the films *My Girl* and *My Girl 2*. She lives in Connecticut, USA.

*Anna Paquin, Dana Delany and Jeff Daniels
in the film* Fly Away Home.

Fly Away Home

a novel by

PATRICIA HERMES

from the screenplay by
Robert Rodat and Vince McKewin

Level 2

Retold by Karen Holmes
Series Editors: Andy Hopkins and Jocelyn Potter

Addison Wesley Longman Limited
Edinburgh Gate, Harlow,
Essex CM20 2JE, England
and Associated Companies throughout the world.

ISBN 0 582 40123 2

First published in the USA by New Market Press 1996
First published in Great Britain by Puffin Books 1997
This adaptation first published by Penguin Books 1998
This edition first published 1998

Typeset by Digital Type, London
Set in 11/14pt Bembo
Printed in Spain by Mateu Cromo, S.A. Pinto (Madrid)

Published by Addison Wesley Longman Limited in association with
Penguin Books Ltd., both companies being subsidiaries of Pearson Plc

Dictionary words:

- Some words in this book are darker black than others. Look them up in your dictionary or try to understand them without a dictionary first, and then look them up later.

Before you read:

1 This story is about young geese in Canada. Find Canada on a map, then find North Carolina. How far is Canada from North Carolina? How far is Canada from your country?
2 What do you know about geese? Where do they live? Why do they fly south in the winter and north in the summer? What do they eat? Find out about them.

Chapter One

I don't remember this place, I thought. It isn't home. Not my home. My home is far away, in New Zealand. With Mum. This is a different home. My dad's home. And I don't like it.

I looked at the house, the **fields** and the heavy rain. No, I didn't remember it. Perhaps I didn't want to remember it. It was an old house, in the centre of wet fields. Rain. It rained the night it happened. The night my mum died. The night the car hit us. I remember I cried, I wanted Mum. And I remember the hospital and the noises in my head.

'When were you last here, Amy?' Dad said quietly. 'Seven years ago?'

I looked through the car window. 'Nine,' I said.

'Oh,' Dad said. 'As long as that.'

Yes, as long as that. It was nine years ago when Mum left Dad and moved away. My mother and I went to live in New Zealand. I was very young then. Sometimes Dad came to us in New Zealand or we came back here to Canada. Not often. But now Mum was dead and I had to stay with him. In this place that wasn't home.

Dad stopped the car. 'Ready?' he asked.

I wasn't. But we ran into the house, into the kitchen. Inside, I stopped and looked at the room. Kitchen? This was a kitchen? This was a **mess**! There were things on the floor. Dad makes **machines**, it's his job.

'I'm very tired,' I said.

He turned and we went up to my room. 'I didn't have time to make your room nice before I came to get you,' he said. 'Everything happened very quickly . . .'

He opened the door. My room. This was my room? It was worse than the kitchen. More things on the floor, the **wing** of an aeroplane, machines, boxes. And in one corner, a bed. For a long

1

Now Mum was dead I had to stay with Dad.

minute, we did not say anything. I walked into the room. How can I sleep here? I thought. Here in this mess? How can he use my room? Doesn't he know ...? I closed my eyes. It happened quickly. He flew to New Zealand, flew there and brought me home, because Mum was ...

'I'll do it tomorrow,' Dad said quietly. 'You'll remember it then.'

'I don't remember it,' I said. I sat down on the bed. This place is a mess, I thought. I don't want to live here – without Mum. I want him to go. Now.

'I'm very tired,' I said.

For a long minute, Dad looked at me. Then he looked at the room again, then back at me. 'OK,' he said quietly. 'Goodnight.'

Do I remember this room? I thought. Did Mum put me to bed here and sing to me? No, I don't remember. I don't remember this house, and I don't remember this room. And I don't remember my father ...

Suddenly I heard somebody speak in the room below. A ... woman! For a minute I thought: Mum!

I jumped up, went to the door, opened it.

But it wasn't Mum. It wasn't a woman. It was Dad, on the phone.

I tried to picture Mum there in the kitchen with him, but I couldn't. Couldn't picture Mum here. I couldn't see Mum's face now.

Chapter Two

Where am I? I thought next morning. Back in the hospital? I looked at the room. I wasn't in the hospital. It was the morning and I was here, in this place, but it wasn't home.

The sun was hot. That was something. No more rain. I got up. Outside I saw a field with flowers, some **hills** and below the hills, a **marsh** with water and **geese**. There was nothing there, only trees and fields and hills, no people or houses. Mum left here because it was very quiet. The only moving things were those geese in the marsh. And then I saw it ... this ... this big thing! Something moving. It was very big, as big as a small plane. What was it?

A man? A man with wings. But people don't have wings, not here in Canada, I knew that.

The thing climbed up the hill, slowly, slowly. Then it stopped and turned. And suddenly, it went running down the hill.

Then I saw it was Dad, my dad. It was my dad with wings, running, running down the hill – and then suddenly he flew through the sky. He flew over the trees and over the house. I ran outside. Yes, I saw him fly over the hill, as big as a bird. He turned and came back. He came in slowly, slowly, to the hill. Then the wind caught him and he suddenly went up again. Then the wind

It was my dad with wings.

stopped and he came down. Hard. Fell again and again, and didn't move.

Dead. He was dead. I knew it. He was **crazy**. And he was dead.

I ran to him, but he suddenly threw off the wings, saw me look at him and laughed. He laughed! He was happy! Happy? He was crazy!

I turned quickly, went back into the house. I didn't want to speak to him. Where to go?

There was this big hill at the back of the house and I went up to it. I looked down at the house and the marsh below. It was quite pretty down there, trees and flowers, and geese on the water of the marsh. There were a lot of geese, some of them on **nests** with their babies.

Is it nice to sit on a nest, to have babies, to teach them to swim and to fly? I thought. Is it interesting? Or hard work? To fly with them, to fly away, then back?

I want to fly away home to Mum. Where was Mum? Was she above me, up in the sky?

4

Crazy, I thought. I stood up, went down the hill to the marsh, stood near the water, and looked at the geese. I stayed there, but the geese were afraid and so I left and went back to the house.

Chapter Three

It was morning and I was up very early, before Dad got up, before it was time for the school bus. I stood at the back door. I'm *not* going to school, I thought. I was at school yesterday and the day before, and I didn't like it there – people laughed at me.

I'll stay in the fields behind the house and come back after the bus goes, I thought. I wanted time to think about things, too. About Susan, my dad's friend. She came to the house last night for dinner. I don't think Susan liked seeing me here. Bad luck, I lived here now.

When I went up to bed I heard her say, 'She's different. Difficult to understand.' Difficult? I thought. Why did she think that?

I know Dad wanted her to stay. Did she stay most nights? I didn't know.

'No,' she said. 'I don't think I'll stay. Not with Amy here.'

I looked out of the window. There was a noise. The school bus? I looked at my watch. No, too early. The noise came again. Then I heard a different sound, some geese called, and then the first noise again. What was it? Where was it?

Down by the marsh, I saw something – something big and yellow. A machine. Yes, a machine moving fast, making a lot of noise. It moved and trees fell in front of it. And the geese were afraid, calling, making a lot of noise too.

Then … something happened. Dad. He ran out of the bedroom, past me. He pulled open the door, and ran down the hill with his arms up.

'Stop! Stop!' he cried. 'You can't do this!'

I saw him throw something at the machine. He was crazy. Mum left him because he was crazy!

I ran up to my room and put on my jeans and a shirt. I'm leaving here, I thought. Away from this crazy man. But where can I go? Not to school.

Suddenly the noise stopped. I listened. Nothing. It was very quiet, inside and outside.

'Amy?' It was Dad. 'Sorry about that. These people want to build next to our place. We want to stop them. I told the driver of the machine to stop for now but . . .'

'It's not my problem,' I said. 'See? It's not my problem, not any of it.'

He looked at me.

'And I'm not going to school again,' I cried.

He opened his mouth, closed it.

And you're crazy! This place is crazy! I don't like you! I want Mum. I didn't say the words, because suddenly, I started to cry. I fell on the bed, face down, and cried.

'Amy?' Dad said. He came and stood next to the bed.

'Why did all this happen?' I said.

No answer. But I knew Dad was there.

'Why can't I get up in the morning and find everything is OK?' I asked. He didn't answer.

I couldn't stop crying. 'Tell me,' I said. I turned and looked at him. I wanted to sit up and . . . do something. Hit him. Mum was dead. I wanted her, not him.

Dad put out his hand to me. He opened his mouth to say something. But then he closed it. He didn't say a word. He stood there, one hand out.

I turned away. After a long minute, I heard him leave. I heard him go out, heard the door close quietly behind him. He didn't understand. He didn't love me.

Chapter Four

I went to school that day. It was better than staying at home and waiting for the next crazy thing. I didn't speak all day, not on the bus to school, not in school, not on the bus home, not a word.

I went home and walked back to the marsh. The yellow machine was not there, but it had left a mess. And there were no geese. I stood quietly and looked all round, but I didn't see any geese.

Then suddenly I saw something. **Eggs** – a nest of them. Six eggs in a nest, six beautiful eggs. But no mother **goose**. I looked at the marsh again. No mother. No father. Where were they? Dead? Or afraid? Will they come back? I thought.

I was there for a long time, a very long time. But I didn't see or hear one goose.

I looked at the eggs. How will they live without a mother to warm them? For a long time, I stood there. I'll find a place for them, I thought, a warm place . . .

No, I can't. Nobody can be their mother.

But why not? I thought. I must make a warm place for them, then they'll live . . . No, I can't.

Then I thought about my mum. I thought about her, and I heard her speak to me in my head. Why not? I heard her say. Who says you can't do it, Amy? I think you'll be a very good mum.

I smiled and looked at the eggs. Can I be their mother? Can I find – or make – a place for them? Where? My room? No. Dad will be angry. In the garage? Yes, the garage is best. I looked at the eggs again. 'I'll be back,' I said to them. Then I ran to the garage.

I got there and stopped. Can Dad help? No. He'll say no, he'll say school is more important . . . Better not say anything.

In the garage I looked for a warm, quiet place. I looked at the table. There was a cupboard under it. Yes, the cupboard will be warm.

I found an old baby's dress and took it back to the marsh with me. Down at the marsh, I walked carefully through the water. The eggs were there. Very carefully I began to put them into the old dress. They were cold. The babies are dead! I thought. No, they'll be OK. I'll warm them. 'You're cold now,' I said to them, 'but you'll warm up. You'll be OK.'

After I put them all in the dress, I thought: Are there other nests, other babies without mothers?

Carefully, I walked across the marsh. And I found them! Ten more eggs in different nests.

At every nest, I stopped, then took the eggs. 'You'll be OK,' I told them. 'You'll be OK. I **promise**.'

Sixteen eggs. Sixteen babies without mothers.

In the garage, I made the nicest nest in the cupboard. Then, I started to take the eggs out of the old dress. I put them in the new nest, all sixteen of them. When I finished, I stood up and looked at them. Was it warm in the cupboard?

I found a big light; Dad used it for his work. Carefully, I put the light in the cupboard. Yes! Warm. It got very warm. The babies will love it. They'll think their mum is here. Everything was OK, the light was not too hot or anything. I quietly closed the cupboard door.

'You'll be OK now,' I said to them. 'I promise. Your mum's not here but you're going to be OK.'

Chapter Five

Next day, I thought about my eggs all through school and all through dinner, too. Were they warm? Were they too warm? Were they eggs or baby birds now?

I wanted to look at them in the morning. I went quietly down to the kitchen. Then I heard something behind me. A man sat up in the chair.

Very carefully I began to put them into the old dress.

'Who are you?' I cried.

'Oh. I'm David. You're Amy. I gave you a book for your birthday years ago. You ate it.'

I looked at him. Dad came into the room behind me.

'Who is he?' I asked. 'Why's he here?'

'He's my brother, David,' Dad said. 'He helps me with my work.'

The school bus came and Dad threw me out of the door. 'You must go to school, Amy,' he said. 'Every day.'

'Wait,' I said but he didn't listen. I went. It was the longest day. Now it was late afternoon and I was home. Dad and Susan were out but I couldn't go and look at the eggs because of David. We sat at the dinner-table together.

'David,' I said, 'I don't want any more dinner. I want to . . .'

'Why does your dad fly? Do you know?' David asked.

'I'm going out,' I said.

'He started to fly because of Odd Job,' David said. 'That was the name of an old goose that lived at our house.'

I looked at him. 'Dad liked geese?' I said.

'Don't know, but he liked Odd Job. Odd Job was crazy. Somebody cut his wings and he couldn't fly, but he didn't understand that. He ran down this big hill behind the garage. He ran and ran and ran and jumped into the sky, then fell down again. Then he tried again.'

David got up, went over and sat in front of the TV. 'Crazy,' he said. 'Your dad flies because of Odd Job.' Soon he went to sleep in front of the TV. Now I could leave!

In the garage, I opened the cupboard door. The eggs moved. I watched them and they moved. I heard the noise they made. They tried to break out!

I was afraid to move, afraid to make a noise. The eggs jumped . . . and jumped . . . and began to open – all of them! Then I saw it – an eye! One big eye looking at me. Slowly, I put a finger on its little head. 'Look at you,' I said.

The eggs jumped and moved. It took a long time, a very long time but they did it – they opened! My eggs. My eggs were little geese.

'You are beautiful,' I said. 'All of you.'

I stood there for a long time and looked at them. A long, long time.

Then suddenly I knew I couldn't leave them there. I had to stay with them. I made a big nest on the floor and put them in it, one by one. It was late, very late. I was very tired and I sat down in the nest next to them. I watched them and they walked over me, over my arms and legs and face.

Names, I thought. I'll give them names. Sixteen names for sixteen babies. Frederica was a good name. Which geese have boys' names and which have girls' names? Long John. That was a good name. And Ralph. Yes. Ralph, the goose.

I smiled at the goose next to me on the floor. 'Muffy,' I said. 'That's a good name for you.'

That's the last thing I remember . . .

'Amy!' Dad stood over me. 'Amy, I didn't know where you were.' He took off his coat, put it over me. 'Are you very cold?' he asked.

I pulled the coat over the geese but it was no good. Dad saw them.

'They . . . they're geese,' I said.

Dad was quiet for a minute. 'Yes. I see,' he said.

'Can . . . can they stay?' I asked.

For a long minute he looked at me. Then he put a hand on my head. 'Why not?' he smiled and said, 'Why not?'

Chapter Six

I brought all the geese into the kitchen. I had to give them food every two hours. They ate it and walked in it and sat in it – the kitchen was a mess!

'They can't stay in the house,' Dad said.

'They must!' I said. 'They're too young to go outside.'

There was a sound outside – the school bus. 'That's your bus!' Dad said.

'I'm not going!' I said.

'Amy!' Dad said.

'Promise me you'll give them food,' I said. 'Every two hours. And promise you won't put them outside.'

'OK, OK, I promise,' Dad said. 'I promise. I promise.'

I looked at my little geese. 'I'll be back,' I said. 'Are you sure you can feed them?' I asked Dad.

He opened the door. 'Go!'

I thought about my geese all day, but they were OK. Dad gave them food and he went to see Glen. Glen worked with animals and birds. Glen promised he'd come to the house and look at the geese.

Every day, Dad and David gave the geese food, and then after school I played with them. They were only little, but they could walk and run. And they followed me. They followed me all the time – sixteen little geese. They followed me through the house and across the fields. Susan and David liked them. And Dad? He was a little angry with them because they made a mess in the house.

'Have they got names?' David asked.

'Most of them,' I said. 'That's Frederica. And that's Long John and Stinky. And there's Ralph and Muffy.'

David looked at the smallest goose, the goose with a bad leg. 'What's his name?' he asked.

I brought all the geese into the kitchen.

'I don't know. He was born with a bad leg. I think I'll call him Igor.'

After dinner, Glen came to the house. He sat and talked to Dad and Susan.

'The geese follow Amy all the time,' Dad said.

'They saw you first and they think you're their mother,' Glen said. 'Now, I must cut their wings so they can't fly. When geese live in people's houses they must not fly.' He picked up a goose.

'No!' I said. 'Put him down, please. They're my geese.'

Glen smiled at me. 'Are you Amy? You see, Amy, I won't **hurt** them, but they must not fly.'

He had Muffy in his hands. Then I hit Glen over the head, hard, with a plate. Then Dad ran across and hit him too. I took Muffy and all the other geese and ran into the bathroom. I heard the fight outside.

'What are you doing?' Dad cried.

'I wanted to help!' Glen said. 'What do you think will happen to these birds? They have no mother and no father. Who'll show them where to go? They'll try to **migrate** and they'll all be dead a month later.'

'No, you won't,' I said to the geese. 'Don't listen to him.'

'Listen to me,' Glen said to Dad. 'If these geese are ill and they fly, they'll make other geese ill. That can't happen. I must cut their wings.'

'Get out!' Dad cried. 'Don't come back here again.'

'If those birds fly,' Glen said, 'I'll take them away.'

'Get out!' Dad cried. I heard the door close.

Glen's leaving, I thought. He'll come back but he's not having my geese. I'll stay here! We'll never leave the bathroom!

Chapter Seven

All night I stayed in the bathroom. I made a bed in the bath. Glen's coming back, I thought. He'll come back in the dark, into the house. But he can't get into the bathroom.

Dad and Susan were very angry. Dad talked to me through the door. 'Nobody's going to hurt your geese,' he said.

Later I heard him tell Susan that he was a bad father. He was always a bad father. And I heard something — something that helped me understand Susan a little better.

She and Dad went outside. I heard them through the bathroom window.

'I'm not a very good father,' Dad said, and Susan answered, 'Well, you're *here*. I never saw my father. He left . . . when I was a little baby.' I was sad. It's sad not to know your father.

I slept. Next thing I knew it was morning. I looked at my little geese. Some of them wore in the bath with me. Thirteen, fourteen, fifteen . . . one goose wasn't there! Igor. Where was Igor?

'Igor!' I said. Then I saw him. He was behind me.

'You crazy thing,' I said, and I put him in the bath with his brothers and sisters.

I climbed into the bath and washed my face. My father had a **soap** machine. The soap came out very fast, into my eyes! And it didn't stop!

I couldn't see. My eyes hurt and I couldn't move because my geese were on the floor.

'Help!' I cried. 'Help me!'

Suddenly Dad was outside. 'Amy! Amy' he said. 'What is it? Open the door!'

'I can't!' I cried. I heard Dad break through the door. He and Susan ran in. I stood there in the bath and cried. Susan put her arms round me. 'It's OK,' she said. 'It's OK.'

'It's not!' I said. I started to cry again. 'I don't like it here! I don't like this crazy house. Dad's crazy. I want my mum. I want my friends. And that Glen man. Dad brought him here. He wants to cut their wings off!'

'Hush,' Susan said. 'Your dad didn't know.'

'He'll come back and get them,' I said.

'Amy,' Susan said. She put her arms round me. 'Now listen to me. Can you listen? I can't be your mother. Nobody can. I don't want to be your mother. But I can be your friend. Let's be friends. And I promise nothing is going to happen to your geese. That's a promise.'

'How can you promise that?' I asked.

'I can,' she said. 'OK? I promise.'

I sat next to her on the floor. It was – it was good.

Chapter Eight

Things were better after that. School finished. Glen did not come back. And, Susan was OK.

They followed me all the time.

But the best, the very, very best thing, was my little geese. They were beautiful and clever, and they followed me all the time. They followed me across the fields and the marsh. I took Dad's bicycle and they followed me. I went fast and the geese ran after me. For weeks we played all day long. We swam together. I was never without my geese. Through the summer, I had friends.

But I was afraid. When is Glen coming back? I thought. He'll hurt my little geese. He'll try and take them away. I watched for him every day.

One night, Susan, David, Dad and I sat in the house and talked. 'What are we going to do in the winter?' Dad said. 'They can't stay here in Canada, it's too cold. There's no food for them.' Then suddenly he cried. 'I know!'

'What?' I said.

'They can follow my aeroplane.'

'They follow the bicycle, right?' Dad said.

'Yes,' I said.

'Then they can follow my aeroplane. I can take them to the States for the winter. Go south. It's warmer there. Geese remember things well. I'll take them down to the States for the winter and they'll fly back here next spring.'

I looked at him. My geese? He wanted to take my geese away? 'No,' I said. 'They're not going to the States. They're staying here with me.'

'Where do you want to take them?' Susan asked.

'To a warm place,' Dad said. 'They can fly there fast.'

'You can't do that!' I said. I was very angry. 'You promised! You promised they'll stay here.'

'I promised and I won't break that promise. But they won't stay here in winter. They'll fly away, they'll migrate. Or we cut their wings, then they'll never fly.'

'They're birds!' I said. 'They must fly!'

Dad looked at me. 'Yes,' he said.

'Oh,' I said. I closed my eyes for a minute. 'I don't know . . . I want them to stay. They want to stay!'

'They'll go,' Dad said. 'You know that. But your geese don't know the south. They must have a mother and a father, to teach them. But they don't have a mother and father. Only me and you. I want to teach them.'

'They won't follow you,' I said.

'I can try,' Dad said. 'If you help me.'

'No,' I said. 'This is crazy. You'll kill them all.'

I went out and sat in the field with the geese. 'You won't go?' I said to Long John. 'Promise you won't go.'

Suddenly I saw that he was very big. I looked at Igor. He was big, too. They were all bigger, not just Long John, but all of them. A lot bigger. They weren't yellow now, they were white. And they wanted to fly. That morning, when I went on the bicycle, they half ran, half flew behind me. Igor tried, but he wasn't very good.

'Must you go?' I said to them.

I turned because I heard somebody behind me. Susan. She sat next to me and took Igor. She didn't say anything. After a minute, I said, 'Do you think they'll fly away?'

'Yes, Amy, you know that.'

'But . . .' I said.

'What?' she said.

'Nothing. But . . . you heard Dad's plan? You know he's crazy. Can it work? Or are they all going to get killed? Dad too?'

Susan laughed. 'Amy,' she said. 'When your dad says he can do something, he usually can.'

I looked at Muffy. 'You must fly south,' I said.

For a long time I sat there and thought. She was right. Dad and David were right. 'OK,' I said. 'Tell him it's OK. We'll try.'

Chapter Nine

The first thing we taught the geese was to follow Dad. We started in the field. They stood behind the bicycle and Dad got on it. He started to move across the field. I ran next to him and all the geese ran after me. Then Dad went faster and they followed him. We did that for days. They learned very fast.

Dad and his friend Barry built a small aeroplane that could fly for hundreds of miles. The geese liked it and the noise it made. Only Igor had a problem. He ran, but he was very slow. And he never got into the sky. He'll never fly, I thought. But the others did. They could all fly.

Then the day came when we took out the aeroplane. Dad didn't want to go far. I didn't want them to leave the house but I wanted them to fly.

Dad started the aeroplane and it flew into the morning sky. Up and up.

I looked up at the plane. The geese looked at the plane too. 'See that?' I said. 'Think you can do it?'

They looked up at the sky. They knew.

Dad brought the aeroplane down again.

'You can do it,' I said. I wanted to cry. 'You can do it. Remember, you're born to fly.'

Dad and Barry built a small aeroplane.

'OK,' I said. 'This is it. First time. It's your big day. Do you understand?'

They all made a noise. They understood. I turned and ran to the plane. They followed me, running fast, some of them half-flying. Very slowly, Dad took the plane off the field. I turned back to my geese, 'Go!' I cried. 'Go! Fly away!' They looked at the sky. Up at Dad in the plane. They moved their wings and they ran. But not Igor. He stopped, turned round and looked at me.

'Go, Igor!' I said. 'Go!'

Dad was up now, above the trees, but the geese were not with him. All sixteen geese were down in the field. They stood and looked up, afraid. They watched Dad and the plane, but they didn't follow. They only looked. After a minute they turned and ran to me.

'What are you doing?' I cried. 'Bad geese! You must fly. Stay here and Glen will cut your wings.'

They looked at me.

Dad came and we tried again. And again — and again. Every time Dad got up in the sky in his plane and the geese stayed in the field. At last Dad stopped the plane.

'We'll try again tomorrow. It takes time for them to learn,' he said.

I wanted to cry. I don't want them to leave but now I'm afraid they'll stay, I thought. I took the geese back to the garage. 'You're crazy,' I said to them. 'Glen's right. You're crazy.'

They ran round my legs. Then I thought — they're children, my children. And I'm their mother. They won't follow Dad, but they'll follow their mother . . .

I looked at the plane. No. Yes? I turned and looked at Dad and Susan. They talked but did not look at me or the plane. I turned to the geese. 'OK, you geese,' I said quietly. 'But this time you fly.'

Chapter Ten

I ran up the hill to the plane and all the geese followed me. I was a little afraid, but I thought I could fly the plane. I watched Dad a lot.

The geese and I were behind the trees. Dad couldn't see us. I climbed in the plane and put on Dad's hat.

I looked at the geese. They watched me. They were quiet, they did not make a noise. They knew this was important. 'Now, follow!' I said. 'Up! Ready? You can do it.'

I started the plane. Slowly, slowly, it began to move. Then it went faster but it didn't move into the sky. Then suddenly it moved very fast and I was up! I did it! I turned and looked back. The geese were behind me. They ran fast, very fast. And then . . . yes! They flew. Not far above the field, but they flew!

I watched them. They were up now. Four, five, six of them, behind me. I heard the sound of their wings.

I flew. They flew. They were in the sky, behind me.

Where was Igor? I looked down. Dad ran quickly across the field.

'It's OK,' I cried. Then suddenly the plane stopped. It started to go down.

There was no sound. Am I going to die? I thought. That was the last thing I remember.

I opened my eyes. Was I dead? Somebody was next to me.

'Amy, Amy, talk to me.'

Dad. It was Dad. Why was he here? He started to cry.

'Hullo,' I said.

'Amy, are you hurt? I thought you were . . .'

'Are you angry?' I asked.

'No, I'm not angry,' Dad said. 'You're OK. That's the most important thing.'

'Dad?' I said. 'Did you see it? They flew with me. They flew with me, Dad. It was beautiful.'

'I know,' Dad said quietly. 'I know.'

Chapter Eleven

Next day, Dad flew again but the geese didn't follow him. He tried again and again and again, but they didn't go up with him. I'll fly, I thought. I know they'll follow me.

I was sad and angry. Dad was sad, David and Susan were sad. The geese were unhappy. They walked round and made a lot of noise. We must cut their wings, I thought.

One night I talked to Mum inside my head. I told her everything. I do that sometimes and sometimes it helps. 'Am I a good mother for the geese?' I asked her. 'I don't think I am. I'm not a good mother.'

Sometimes she answered me in my head. This time she didn't. She wasn't there.

I went back to the house. Susan and Dad were angry.

'You're crazy!' Susan cried.

'No,' Dad said. 'I'm not. See, the birds will fly with Amy. And she'll fly with me. We'll all go south.'

'You want her to fly a plane?' Susan said. 'She's a child!'

'I can do it, Dad,' I cried. 'I can! Let me!'

'We can do it,' David said. 'We'll build a small plane.'

'You're crazy, too,' Susan cried. She ran out of the house.

Dad and David looked at me. I put my hands to my head. Why does this happen? I thought. We find a way to migrate the geese – and I'm unhappy because Susan is angry. I understood then that Susan was important to me. I ran after her. 'Susan,' I said. 'Susan, I know you don't want me to go, but . . .'

'No,' Susan said. 'It's not that I don't want it. But I'm afraid for you.'

22

'I know,' I said. 'But help me. OK?'

'Amy,' Susan said. 'It's dangerous. Think about your mum. She's not here, but . . .'

'I think about her all the time,' I said. 'I tell her everything. About the geese and about them not flying with Dad. I think she wants me to try.'

For a minute Susan closed her eyes. Then she opened them. 'OK,' she said quietly. 'I'll help you.'

Chapter Twelve

Dad and David worked all day and all night for a week and built my plane. At last it was ready. It was beautiful. It had a goose's head and the wings were goose's wings. My geese will love this, I thought.

I was very excited and a little afraid. But I didn't want Dad to see I was afraid.

I sat in the plane. 'OK,' Dad said. 'We're going to do this very slowly.'

He gave me a radio. 'You can talk to me with this,' he said. Then he sat behind me in the plane. 'If you want help, I'm here.'

The plane began to move across the field. We went slowly. It was slow, but it was very exciting. I looked at Dad and smiled. He smiled back.

Every day we moved the plane across the field but we didn't fly. Then the day came when we went up into the sky. We were up! We moved left and right, up and down, went round the field.

'You're doing well,' Dad said. 'I'm not doing anything!'

I flew for a long time. All the time I thought about my geese. I knew they watched me from the field. They looked up, ready to fly with me.

Soon, I thought. Soon we'll go. I'm going to fly away south

'You're doing well,' Dad said.

with you so you can learn about going south in the winter. Then, in spring, you'll come back to me. We're going to do it. We are. Wait and see.

Chapter Thirteen

The day came. Dad let me fly without him. We put the geese in the house. I didn't want them to fly with me today.

'Remember everything I taught you. I'm in my plane behind you,' Dad said. His friend Barry was with him.

'You're good,' Barry said. 'I watch a lot of people fly and you can do it.'

I looked at the floor. Barry liked me! He thought I could fly.

Dad got into his plane and spoke to me on the radio. 'Are you there, Mother Goose?' he asked. 'It's time to go.'

I started the plane. It moved faster and faster and suddenly I was in the sky. Up in the sky! I smiled. I was flying!

'This is good, Father Goose,' I said to Dad on the radio. He didn't answer. I looked back at his plane – and there, behind my plane, I saw Long John!

Long John moved up next to my wing. Long John and . . . All the geese flew behind me, in a long line.

'They left the house,' Dad said. 'They want to fly with you today.'

I heard Barry on the radio. 'There's one unhappy goose down here,' he said. I looked down. Fifteen geese were behind me but one goose wasn't there.

'Oh no, Dad!' I cried. 'We forgot Igor!'

'Let's go back and get him,' Dad said. Slowly I turned the plane and the geese went with me. I saw Igor in the field, saw him look up. Saw him run.

'Come on, Igor!' I cried. 'Come on!'

Igor ran fast, then faster. Suddenly he was up in the sky.

'He can fly, Dad!' I cried.

The geese followed me. They looked beautiful. I smiled but I wanted to cry. And I thought my Mum smiled, too.

Chapter Fourteen

Suddenly it was autumn. I went back to school. I didn't like it. Glen came to my school every Tuesday and talked about birds to the students. I didn't like him.

Every day, after school, we flew with the geese. We made them

'They want to fly with you today.'

strong for their journey. They had to fly two hundred miles every day for four or five or six days.

They were good. All but Igor. He was no good at flying. He fell, he was always the last in the sky and the first to come down again. I was afraid for him.

Dad and David talked to this man, Dr Killian. 'There's a marsh for the geese in North Carolina,' he said. But we had to get them there before November the 1st.

'After November the 1st, builders want to move in and build on the marsh,' Dr Killian said. 'The geese get there first, then the builders can't build there.'

'You and I will fly with the geese,' Dad said to me.

'Susan, David and Barry will follow us with a car and a boat and they'll bring our food. Every night we'll bring the planes down and meet them.'

We were ready. Only Igor was a problem.

One day I was with the geese. I heard something, looked up and there was Glen.

'What do you want?' I asked.

'I want to see your dad.'

'He's not here,' I said. 'Go away.'

Glen smiled. 'Your geese can fly. I heard your dad has a crazy plan. I'll be back.' He left the house.

'Don't be afraid,' I told the geese. 'Two more days and we'll be out of here.'

Later, Dad and I flew with the geese. Barry called me on the radio. 'There's a goose down here,' he said.

I looked down. It was Igor.

'He must come with us, Field Goose,' I said to Barry. 'Put the radio next to Igor.'

'OK, Mother Goose,' Barry said. I heard Igor through the radio.

'Listen to me, Igor,' I said. 'This isn't good. Tomorrow we leave. You must fly or Glen will cut your wings.'

Suddenly Igor understood. Perhaps he was afraid of Glen. He jumped into the sky and moved his little wings.

'He's up, Mother Goose,' Dad said.

'I see him!' I said.

I turned and looked behind me. All the geese were there. Igor was there. Next minute, we lost him again!

'Father Goose,' I called into the radio. 'I can't see him.'

We turned back to home.

'Wait, Amy!' Dad said. 'Here he comes!'

I turned, looked. Igor. He flew into the wing of my plane!

I saw him fall down to the field.

'Dad!' I cried. 'Dad, I hit him. Daddy, I hit Igor. He's down.'

I began to cry.

'Amy,' Dad said. 'Look behind you!'

I turned, saw my geese, all my other geese behind me.

'You must help them, Amy,' Dad said. 'Get them home. Turn and go home. Now. Do you understand? You must help them!'

Yes, I understood. I cried, but I did it. I turned the plane and they followed me. All but Igor.

Chapter Fifteen

All day and night Barry, David, Susan, Dad and I walked round and looked for Igor. We didn't find him.

We looked for hours before it was dark. I started to cry. Susan took my hand. Then I heard David say, 'Look at this! Look at this!'

'What?' I said.

He stood and looked at the field. There was a lot of noise and suddenly Igor walked out of the marsh.

'Igor!' I cried. I ran to him. 'Is he OK?' I asked.

'Yes, I think he's OK,' Dad said. 'But not his wing. He won't fly for a day or two.'

'He must,' I said.

'Let's take him home. We'll think of something,' Dad said.

I carried Igor home, made him warm with my arms. I talked to him all the time. 'The other geese were afraid, too. But you're OK now. We'll help you fly again.'

It was very quiet near the house. Where were the other geese? I looked for them. They weren't there!

I ran back to the house and told Dad. 'Glen must have them,' he said. 'They didn't want to leave here.'

'He'll cut their wings.'

'No,' Dad said. 'It will take a long time because they're big now. We'll get them back.'

By morning, Dad and David and Barry had a plan. They went to Glen's house and saw the geese were there.

'Tomorrow is Tuesday,' Dad said. 'Glen goes to your school on Tuesdays, he's not at home. You're going to fly your plane over his house and the geese will see you and follow you.'

Was Dad right? Was it going to be easy? Dad made me think it was. And I wanted the plan to work.

Chapter Sixteen

Next morning Susan, Barry and David were ready with the little boat and car. Everything was ready.

We must get the geese back, I thought. And how can I take Igor with us when they migrate? How? Then I thought of it. The old baby's dress! I'll put the dress round Igor then he can't fly and he can sit in the plane with me!

It was time to go. Dad took my hand. 'It's going to be OK,' he said. 'We're going south. You can do it. I know you can.'

We said goodbye to Susan, got in the planes and started to fly.

Next morning Susan, Barry and David were ready
with the little boat and car.

We flew over Glen's house. I heard my geese, they called to me. I knew they could hear my plane.

David went to Glen's house and opened the door in the garden. It took a long time. I thought something was wrong. I turned the plane and flew back over the house again. I saw the geese down there, and suddenly they saw me and started to fly! They climbed into the sky after me. First one goose, then a second and a third. Fifteen geese.

'See that, Igor!' I said. 'They're here! We can fly away!'

I flew away from Glen's house, over my school, then looked at the geese. They were all there, with Long John at the front. I saw Dad's plane.

'We did it!' I said on my radio.

'It's going to be a long day,' Dad said. 'We must fly a hundred and twenty miles before tonight, then we go over into the States.'

'It'll be OK,' I said. I looked at my geese. They flew near the wing of my plane.

'Going home,' I told them. 'Going south. You were born to do this.'

Chapter Seventeen

We flew all day and into the night across Lake Ontario. I was tired and I knew Dad was tired, too. And the geese were tired.

I called Dad. 'Father Goose. We have some tired geese here.'

'Five more minutes,' Dad said.

I heard him call Barry in the boat below. 'Water Goose,' he said. 'We must come down.'

It was dark. How can we go down in the dark? I thought. Then I saw lights. We brought the planes down near the lights. Suddenly there were two more planes next to us, black planes. There were more black planes in the field.

'Dad,' I said. 'What is this?'

I looked for my geese. They were there.

'Don't move!' somebody cried. 'Hands up!'

I looked at Dad. 'Do it, Amy,' he said.

There were men near us, men with guns. I was afraid.

'Dad,' I said. 'What is this place?'

'It's OK,' Dad said. We **held** hands. The men with guns took us to an office. Inside there was a very angry man.

'What are you doing?' he cried. 'This is an important airport. You can't come down here!'

'We had to, sir,' Dad said.

'We're sorry, sir,' I said.

'Sorry?' he cried. 'Sorry? This is very bad. You can't stay here.'

He looked at me for a long time. What's he going to do to us? I thought. Call the police?

'We promise we won't do it again,' I said.

Then the man began to laugh. I looked at Dad and he smiled at me. I looked at the man. Was it OK now?

A second man came in. 'I write for the newspaper,' he said. 'Tell me about the geese and the planes. And I want a photograph of you and the geese.'

After that, the people at the airport were very good to us. They gave us food and a place to sleep. And they gave food to the geese. Next morning, there were more people from the newspapers and the television. They took lots of photographs and talked to us about the geese. Then we got into the planes again and left.

Barry called us on the radio. 'Listen to this,' he said. We heard people talk, people from the TV and radio. It was all about us! About me and Dad and the geese.

We heard somebody say, 'Look for the two planes and the geese. You see them, you tell us!'

'Listen, Dad,' I said. 'Everybody knows about us. People are looking for us.'

Next morning we got into the planes again and left.

I turned and looked at the geese. We're going to get there, I thought. We're going to do it. Dad was right. He promised and he was right.

Chapter Eighteen

By late afternoon, my geese were tired again, but I knew we must fly on. We had to get them to the marsh in North Carolina.

'Dad,' I said into the radio. 'Everybody's very tired.'

'Ten miles,' Dad said. 'Not far.'

Suddenly in front of us we saw a lot of new geese.

'Daddy! Look!' I cried. Then I saw something that made me afraid. Long John, my strongest and best goose started to follow the new geese. And my other geese all followed Long John.

'Long John!' I cried. 'Come back!' Where are you going?'

'Follow them, Amy,' Dad said.

I turned the plane and followed them. I saw them go down on to some water near a house. Then I heard a gun!

'Bring the plane down, Amy,' Dad said. 'The geese are OK but we must go down.'

I brought my plane down next to Dad's in a field.

'It'll be OK,' Dad said. 'In the morning we'll call them and they'll come with us.' Then we heard the gun again. An old woman walked over to us, a gun in her hands.

'Crazy,' I said to Dad. 'Two times in two days.'

'You people are killers!' the old woman cried. 'You want to catch these geese. You want to kill them!'

'No,' Dad said. 'You don't understand. We're . . .'

'Nobody kills geese at my place,' she said angrily.

Then Igor walked out of the plane. I held him.

The woman looked at him, then looked at Dad, then at me. 'Wait a minute!' she said. 'I know you! You're the little girl with the geese. And that's Igor. I saw you on TV.'

'Yes,' I said. 'It's Igor.'

She smiled. 'Oh, right! You can sleep here,' she said. 'I'm Mabel. You can stay with me.'

After dinner we watched television. Mabel was right. We were all on TV.

I was very tired. Flying was exciting but it was hard work. And in the plane I had a lot of time to think. I thought a lot about Dad. About Mum. About me and my geese.

Dad phoned Susan. 'The geese are with some new geese,' he told her.

'It's good for them,' Susan said. 'They can fly with the other geese.'

'No,' I said. 'I don't want the geese to fly away now. We must get them to the marsh, to the right place. Then they'll come back to me next spring.'

Later we heard something on the TV. 'The geese are going to a marsh in North Carolina. But the day after tomorrow a builder will start to build new houses on the marsh. The geese must be there by tomorrow evening. The geese must get there first, then nobody can build on the marsh.'

'Tomorrow?' I asked. 'Can we do it?'

'Yes,' Dad said. 'It'll be hard, but we'll get there before they start to build on the marsh.'

I walked out of the house. I heard the geese out there in the dark. Come to me tomorrow, I thought. It's important. At the marsh you'll be happy, but you must get there first.

Dad and I slept in one room. I thought about Dad. He helped me with the geese. Why? Does he . . . love me? Do I love him?

'You OK?' Dad asked.

'Yes,' I said. 'Dad. What happened with you and Mum? She wanted to live in the city and you didn't like the city. You were wrong and she was wrong too.'

'Perhaps we were,' Dad said. 'But we did something right. We had you.'

'But you never came to see us,' I said.

For a minute Dad didn't answer. Then he said, 'It took me a long time. Then I understood I was wrong to lose you and your mum. I was angry and afraid. I knew I hurt you. I'm sorry.' He turned and looked at me. 'I'm very sorry. And I'm happy you're here. Can we . . . start again?'

'Yes,' I said. 'I think we can.'

Chapter Nineteen

Next morning, before it was light, we met David and Barry and Susan and went to find the geese.

'Hey, Long John,' I said quietly, 'come on.'

There was no sound. No Long John. No geese.

'Try again,' Dad said.

'Here, Long John,' I called. 'Here Frederica, here Sam.' I listened. Nothing. There were two hundred geese out there, and my geese were with them. I looked at Igor.

'Can you help?' I asked. He made a lot of noise and suddenly they came to me! They did! My fifteen geese swam out from the two hundred.

'Look!' I said to Dad. 'Look! They did it!'

He smiled. 'Yes, they did it. Let's go. We have a long day in front of us.'

'You have ten hours to get to the marsh,' David said. 'You must fly all day.'

We flew for a long time with the geese behind us. Suddenly we were over a city.

'Daddy!' I called on the radio.

'We're OK,' Dad said. 'Stay near me. We're going over that big street.'

I followed Dad. There were buildings below us. I saw people look up at us. Then we turned the planes and we flew away from there, south.

We flew on all day. It was late afternoon. 'How are you, Amy?' Dad said.

'I'm OK,' I said. 'The geese are too. A little tired.'

'We'll make it,' Dad said. 'About one more hour.'

One more hour and my geese will be free, I thought. We flew over a hill. Then suddenly I heard Dad on the radio.

'Oh no!' he cried. I looked for him and saw his plane fall out of the sky behind me.

'Daddy!' I cried. I called David on the radio. No answer. I saw Dad's plane fall and hit a field.

I looked for a place to bring my plane down. The geese were near me. 'We're going down,' I said. 'Come with me.'

Please let him be OK, I thought. Don't let him be hurt. Don't let him be . . .

I jumped out of my plane. Then I saw him. He was there. Next to a tree.

'Daddy!' I cried. 'Are you OK?'

'My arm,' he said. 'It's not too bad but I hurt my arm. I can't fly. You must take them to the marsh.'

I looked at him. 'Me? I can't.'

'It's only thirty miles,' Dad said. 'One hour. You can do it.'

'I can't.'

'You can. I know you can. You and your mum are the same. She went and followed her **dream**. You can too. This is your dream.'

'I want Mum now,' I said.

'She's here,' Dad said. 'She is. She's next to you. She's in the geese, she's in the sky, she's all around you. She is. And she'll help you.'

'But . . .'

'You must take them to the marsh.'

'Go,' Dad said. 'I want you to take the plane, take those geese and go. Go! There isn't a lot of time!'

I ran back to the plane. I must follow my dream. But I was afraid.

Chapter Twenty

I was very afraid. How can I do this? I thought. How can I find the marsh without Dad?

I took the plane up over the trees. The geese were behind me, Igor next to me in the plane. I flew for a long time. Twenty minutes but I thought it was twenty hours. Where am I? Why wasn't Dad here? And where was Mum? I looked at my watch. Where was the marsh?

I flew over a long street in a town. Suddenly I saw something – people, the people down there in the street of the town – two women. They jumped up and down, moved their arms. Go left! they told me. I turned the plane left and they jumped up and down again. Yes!

'We're near the marsh, geese,' I called to them. 'You're home.'

And then I heard something. A sound. Yes, I heard my mum. 'Goodbye, my love,' I heard her say. 'Goodbye, I'm going away . . . but I'll be back.'

I smiled and cried. Was dad right? Was Mum here? In the sky. The marsh? The geese?

Far away in the evening light, I saw the marsh. Five minutes until the sun went down. And I saw hundreds of TV and newspaper people down there near the marsh.

Slowly, I took the geese down to the water of the marsh, to their new home. Home. My geese were home.

'You're home now,' I said. 'You're home.'

I took Igor out of the plane. He ran to his brothers and sisters. They all knew they were home.

Slowly, I took the geese down to the water of the marsh.

Dad, Susan, Barry and David ran to me. I started to laugh and I cried too. I heard Mum say, 'I'll be back . . .'

'You did it!' Dad said.

I looked at him. 'Yes. And you were right,' I said. 'Mum was there.'

I didn't say anything more. He knew.

Mum was in the sky, in the geese. In the people down in that town. In Susan and Barry and David. She came back. Or perhaps she never went away.

I took Dad's hand. Mum followed her dream. Dad followed a dream too.

And he helped me to follow my dream.

Chapter Twenty-One

The next spring, I heard a sound. It came in the night. I was asleep, but I thought I heard something. It was a small sound at first, something on the water.

And then I knew. Geese!

I opened the window. Yes! Yes!

I started to call for Dad and Susan. But then I stopped. Wait! Not for a minute, I thought. I stood at the window and looked across the field in the night. I smiled. They were back. My geese were back.

EXERCISES

Vocabulary Work

Look back at the 'Dictionary Words' in this book. Do you understand them?

1 Find a dictionary word for each of these phrases.

   a Large birds in this story.

   b You wash your face with this.

   c Part of a bird – or an aeroplane.

   d Birds have their eggs and their young in these.

   e Baby birds are born inside these.

   f When birds fly away and live in a different place, they . . .

   g Open green places – birds and animals live here.

   h Cars, planes and radios are all . . .

   i Small mountains!

   j Wet places near a river or near the sea. Birds often live in these places.

2 Use each of these words in a sentence:

   dream   mess   crazy   hurt   promise

Comprehension

Chapters 1–3

1 What happened to Amy's mother?

2 Who is Susan? Why doesn't Amy like her?

Chapters 4–6

3 What does Amy find in the marsh?

4 Why does Amy take the eggs from the nest?

5 What does she do with them?

6 What does Glen want to do with the geese? Why?

Chapters 7–10

7 What is Amy's father's 'crazy plan'?

8 When Amy flies the plane, what happens to the geese?

Chapters 11–14

9 Why doesn't Susan want Amy to fly?

10 Why must the geese fly to North Carolina before November the 1st?

Chapters 15–18

11 How do Amy and her father get the geese back from Glen's house?

12 Why doesn't the old woman like Amy and her father?

Chapters 19–21

13 What happens to Amy's father in Carolina? Why can't he fly to the marsh?

14 What happens the next spring?

Discussion

1 At first Amy doesn't like her father but later she understands him. Have you ever changed your ideas about somebody? Why?

2 Who is your favourite person in this book? Why?

Writing

Either

You are Amy. Write a letter to a friend in New Zealand and tell him/her about your geese. Write about 150 words.

Or

Amy follows her dream and does something she thinks is very important. What is your dream? Write 150 words about something you want to do. Why do you want to do it?